Photographs: Anna Riwkin-Brick

Text: Vera Forsberg

Gennet lives in Ethiopia

The Macmillan Company · New York

The girl on the horse is Gennet. She lives in Ethiopia, far away in Africa. Everyone there is very fond of riding—especially the children. The mountains were yellow with *mäskel* flowers seven years ago, when Gennet was born. "It is as beautiful as paradise here," her grandmother said. So she was called Gennet, which means "paradise" in Amharic, the language she speaks.

The houses in Gennet's village are round and roofed with grass. "We say *tukul*, not house," says Gennet. "*Tukuls* are good houses, cool in summer and warm in the winter nights. It can be cold in Africa, too, although many people will not believe it. When we do our cooking, the smoke goes out just where the roof and walls meet. People who don't know that sometimes think the whole village is on fire."

"Come to our *tukul* to see my mother. She's just getting dinner ready. We usually have *injera* bread with hot red-pepper sauce. Mother puts onions and sometimes hard-boiled eggs in the sauce. At Lent it is made with vegetables and fish. I like fish, but why does it have so many bones?"

This is Desta, Gennet's best friend. They play together all the time,
except when their mothers want them to mind the babies or collect
firewood. Sometimes their mothers ask them to peel onions for the
pepper sauce. "No, please, Mother," beg Gennet and Desta,
"peeling onions makes our eyes water."

When their mothers ask the girls to fetch water from the stream, they are always willing. They are not allowed to take the big pitchers yet, and the small ones aren't even as heavy as a baby. If they hold the pitchers like this, they can easily carry them up the hill to the village.

Tadesse is Gennet's big brother. He is twelve years old. Hasn't he
a fine hat? He has braided it himself of grass. The cowherds have
promised Tadesse that he can go with them when they drive the
cattle down to the lowlands to graze—if his father will let him,
of course. "Oh, how I'd like to go with them!" he says.

Father doesn't answer at once. He thinks it is a long way to the pastures. Besides, Tadesse is very useful at home on the farm. Then Father remembers how glad he was when *he* was twelve years old and became a cowherd. "Very well," he says at last. "Off you go."

First, all the cows in the neighborhood are collected. People seldom save money and put it in the bank in Ethiopia. They buy cows or horses or donkeys instead. When all the cows are together, they are herded down into the valley, where the ground is still

green and there is plenty of water. But the valley is dangerous, too. It is hot and unhealthy. That is why his mother doesn't want Tadesse to go. "He is only a child," says she. "What if he gets sick down there?"

One day the sliding door of the hut is left open, and Mamo, Gennet's baby brother, creeps out. No one notices anything until he screams. Mother rushes to him just in time to see a snake wriggling away through the grass. It has bitten him. "I think it is a poisonous snake," says Mother, holding Mamo. "He must have medicine as quickly as possible. But who can go to get the doctor? I will have to stay here and keep Mamo quiet and warm; Tadesse has gone to the valley and Father is at the market."

"I can go," says Gennet. Her heart is beating rapidly, for she has never been anywhere alone before. But she has to save Mamo. "If you get lost, don't be afraid to ask the way," Mother cautions. Gennet sets off at once. People look surprised when she runs by so fast. They don't know how important it is for her little brother to have help *soon* for his snakebite.

As she is running through the wood, Gennet hears an awful noise.
"I'd better hide," she thinks. "It may be a lion or a hyena or some
other dangerous animal." But it is only a crowd of monkeys
Gennet has disturbed while they are eating. "I ought to remember
that hyenas hunt at night and it's a long time since lions lived in
our wood."

Then the wood thins and Gennet comes to the bird lake. There
are at least a thousand long-legged flamingos wading in the water.
They are so busy looking for small fish that they forget to be

afraid when Gennet runs past them. "Perhaps they understand that I am afraid, too," she thinks. There are so many birds with long, sharp beaks!

The path from the lake to the doctor's follows a stream with steep
banks and deep water, and Gennet doesn't know how to cross it.
"If only you could help me over," she says to the cows grazing by
the stream. "But all you do is eat. I must hurry. Mamo may die
if I can't get over the stream!"

But there is a boy with the cows. He shows Gennet a place where she can wade across. It is awfully easy when there is someone whose hand she can hold. "Thank you," says Gennet. "I'd go with you," says the boy, "but I can't leave the cows." Gennet runs along the stream. Now it is so shallow that she can walk across anywhere! Lots of people are along its banks. Some women are dyeing cloth a beautiful yellow—as yellow as the *mäskel* flowers. "I *do* wish I had a yellow dress," thinks Gennet.

Gennet runs and runs. The road to the doctor's is by the big tree over there. Or is it another tree? "I had better ask that woman who is selling spices," she thinks, "for I mustn't get lost."

"I hope she's not at home," thinks Gennet as she passes the witch's *tukul*, which stands all by itself in the wood. "She might want to give Mamo magic medicine, and then he'd never get better...."

"How happy that girl looks, carrying her little brother on her back. And I am so tired and hungry. . . . But I mustn't think of that. The most important thing in the world is to get the medicine to make Mamo better again."

"What a hurry you are in, Gennet; stay and play with us," say two little cowherds she meets. "No time," says Gennet. It seems a thousand years since she and Desta were playing together, never thinking about snakes that bite babies. Just then she sees a flock of vultures high up in an acacia tree. "Fly home to our field and you can have a snake for dinner. That will serve the snake right," she adds.

"The doctor is not far away," say the people sitting under the great baobab tree. "Petrus, the teacher at the village school, will show you where he is. He will make sure you don't have to wait."
"Please, teacher, help me," says Gennet.
"Of course," says the teacher. "The doctor must see your brother at once." So he takes Gennet's hand and leads her to the doctor.

"We had better take the jeep," says the doctor when he has heard the whole story. But first he packs the medicine and everything else he needs into his brown bag.

"Hold tight!" he says when they are in the jeep, "we have to hurry." And he drives so fast that trees and people almost fly past —and backward, too.

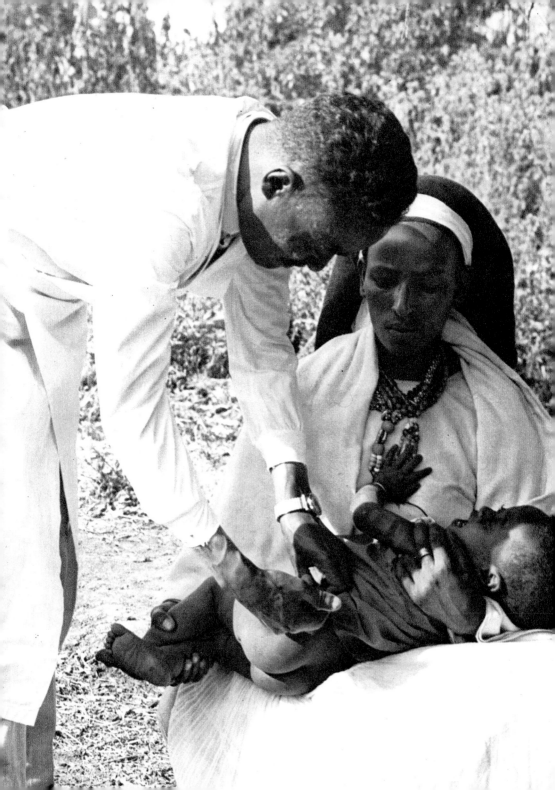

"I'm so glad you're here," says Mother when they get home,
"Mamo is terribly sick."
Mamo cries a little when the doctor gives him his medicine, but
soon he smiles at Gennet, then yawns sleepily. "He'll be better in
a day or so," says the doctor.
One day, when Mamo is quite well again, Grandfather comes for
a visit. "You must wish for something," he says to Gennet when
Mother tells him what she has done. "If it hadn't been for you,
Mamo would be dead now!"

And Gennet says, "I want to go with Father to market and buy a yellow dress. And lots of beads for Desta and me."

"All right," says Grandfather, "I'll pay for everything."

Early one morning Gennet and Father ride to market with a lot of other people. "I hope you will find a really beautiful yellow dress, you were so brave and helpful," says Grandfather.

"It must be as yellow as the *mäskel* flowers," says Gennet. "That is the most beautiful color we know, Grandmother and I."

What a lot of people are at the market! Now and then Gennet is jostled in the crowd. "Little girls should stay at home, and not get in the way at the market," says a woman sitting under a braided parasol, selling wild honey.

"Not when you are buying beads and a dress," thinks Gennet. No matter where they look, they can't find a yellow dress. Gennet tries not to look disappointed. Suddenly, in the middle of the crowd, they see a tailor with a piece of yellow cloth. He makes Gennet a dress while she watches. It does not take him long to sew the dress on his machine. "We ought to have one of those at home," says Gennet. "It sews much faster than Mother can."

Then Gennet sees lots of beads hanging in thick, colorful strands. There are so many shapes and sizes that it is difficult to choose. At last Gennet buys some pink and blue beads for Desta and, for herself, some green, some pale red, and some yellow ones, of course, for yellow is her favorite color. The yellow beads have small white dots all over. "I'll have a yellow necklace in the middle, with a green one on one side and a pale red one on the other. That will be pretty, won't it?"

"No one in the whole world has such a beautiful yellow dress as I
have," says Gennet when she comes home to her mother and
Mamo. "Hold all my beads while I try it on." Everyone in the
village sits around waiting while Gennet goes in to put on the yellow
dress. Desta is there, too. She looks a little sad. But wait a moment,
soon she will get her beads, and then she will be happy again.

Then Gennet comes to the door in her new dress. It shines in the sun like a whole field of yellow *mäskel* flowers. "Oh, Gennet, how beautiful you are," says Desta.